TOP 10 WOMEN ATHLETES

BY ELLEN LABRECQUE

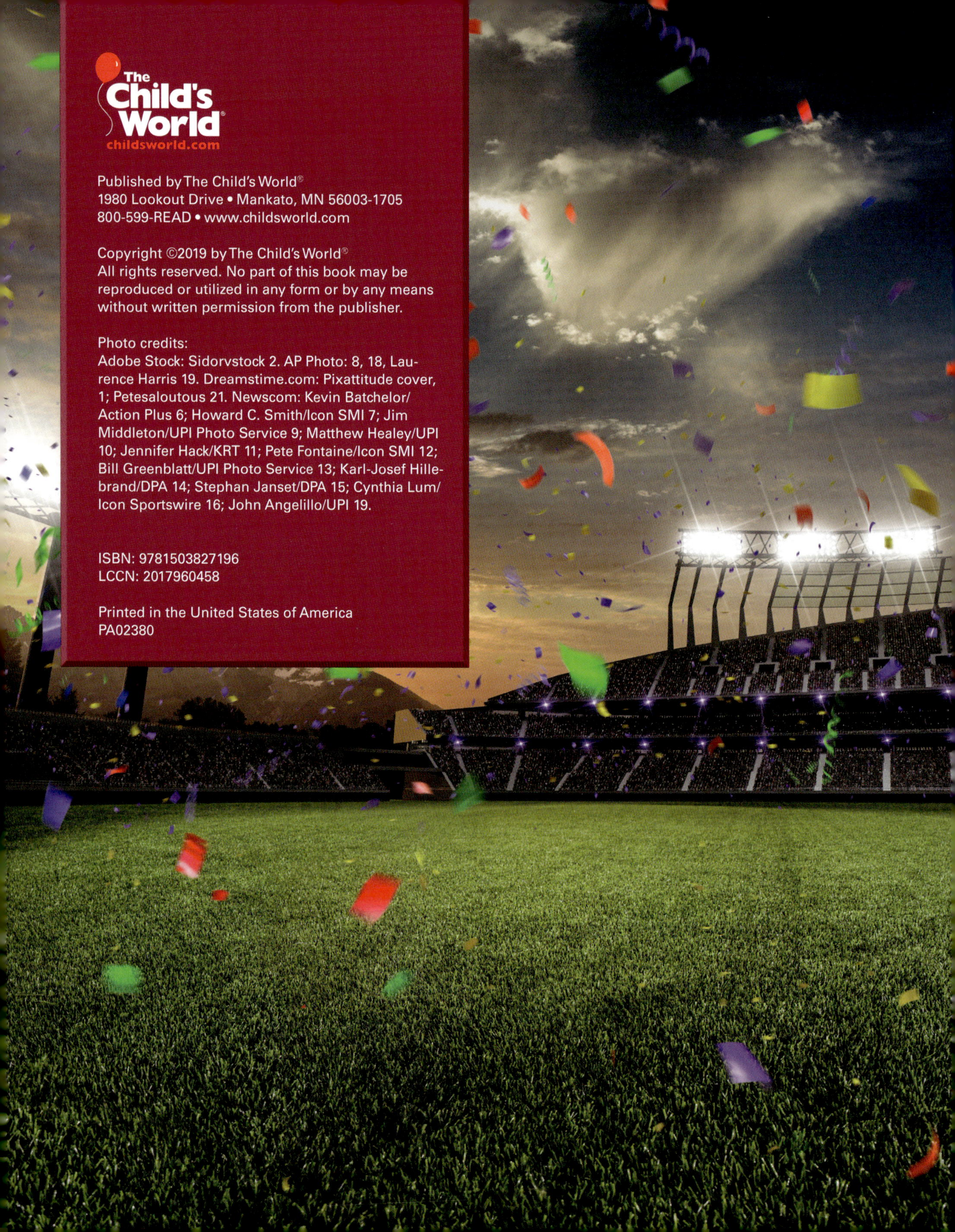

The Child's World
childsworld.com

Published by The Child's World®
1980 Lookout Drive • Mankato, MN 56003-1705
800-599-READ • www.childsworld.com

Photo credits:
Adobe Stock: Sidorvstock 2. AP Photo: 8, 18, Laurence Harris 19. Dreamstime.com: Pixattitude cover, 1; Petesaloutous 21. Newscom: Kevin Batchelor/Action Plus 6; Howard C. Smith/Icon SMI 7; Jim Middleton/UPI Photo Service 9; Matthew Healey/UPI 10; Jennifer Hack/KRT 11; Pete Fontaine/Icon SMI 12; Bill Greenblatt/UPI Photo Service 13; Karl-Josef Hillebrand/DPA 14; Stephan Janset/DPA 15; Cynthia Lum/Icon Sportswire 16; John Angelillo/UPI 19.

ISBN: 9781503827196
LCCN: 2017960458

Printed in the United States of America
PA02380

CONTENTS

WHO'S NUMBER ONE?

At the end of a basketball game, everyone knows who won. It's the team with the most points. At the end of race, the winner is clear. It's the person who crossed the finish line first. Choosing the greatest woman athlete of all time is a bit harder. Is it the athlete who can ski down a mountain as fast as a speeding car? Is it the first woman to dunk a basketball in a pro game? Or the one who won six medals over four different Olympics? Fans, experts, and fellow players all have their opinions.

Babe Didrikson Zaharias

Opinions are different than facts. Facts are real things. Mia Hamm is a two-time World Cup champion. That's a fact. Soccer is the greatest sport in the world. That's an opinion.

The Wimbledon tennis championship is played on grass courts. That's a fact. Serena Williams is the best player to ever compete at Wimbledon. That's an opinion.

Some people might disagree with your opinion. However, they can't say Williams didn't win 23 **Grand Slam** singles titles as of 2017. That's a fact.

Every sports fan has a different opinion: And that's where *you* come in. You get to choose who is the greatest woman athlete ever. You will read lots of facts and stories about these players. Based on that, what's your opinion? Who's No. 1? There are no wrong answers . . . but you might have some fun discussions with your sports-loving pals! Then again, you might just pick the woman who plays your favorite sport . . . it's up to you!

Read on and then after you're done, make your own Top 10 list. Good luck!

Serena Williams

NUMBERS, NUMBERS

Most Summer Olympic Gold Medals won by a Woman

Athlete, Country	Sport	Medals
1. Larisa Latynina, Soviet Union	Gymnastics	9
2. Birgit Fischer, Germany	Canoeing	8
2. Jenny Thompson, U.S.	Swimming	8
4. Vera Caslavska, Czechoslovakia	Gymnastics	7

LUCIANA AYMAR

FIELD HOCKEY

Luciana Aymar ruled her sport like no other. She was nicknamed *La Maga*, the Magician. She dribbled the ball with her stick as if it was attached by string. She was lightning fast, flying by defenders. She could blow past four defenders in a row to score a goal.

Aymar played field hockey since she was seven years old. She was named the world Player of the Year eight times. She led her home country of Argentina to two World Cup titles (2002, 2010). She also won two silver medals and two bronze medals! In Argentina, Aymar is as popular as a movie star. There is a stadium named after her and a **documentary** about her.

She played her last game in December 2014. She led Argentina to a win over Australia. That gave her six Hockey Champions Trophies. Her fans cheered one more time before the Magician disappeared!

Aymar was born in Rosario, Argentina. That's also the birthplace of international soccer star Lionel Messi.

NUMBERS, NUMBERS

Aymar was the flag bearer for Argentina at the 2012 Olympics in London. She was only the second field hockey player ever to have this honor.

MIA HAMM

SOCCER

Hamm is the only woman inducted into the World Football Hall of Fame.

Millions of young soccer players wanted to be like Mia Hamm. She was the first global star of women's soccer. Hamm led the U.S. National Team to the World Cup title in 1991. That was the first World Cup ever held for women. In 1999, the United States hosted the tournament. The final match was U.S. vs. China. More than 90,000 people watched at the Rose Bowl in California. The U.S. team won in a **penalty shootout**. Hamm made one of the shots to help her team to victory.

At age 15, Hamm was the youngest player ever to make the U.S. National Team. She led the University of North Carolina to four college championships. In the 1996 Olympics, Hamm led her team to the gold medal. She also earned gold in 2004.

Hamm retired in 2004. She scored 158 goals in international games. At the time, that was most by anyone, male or female.

NUMBERS, NUMBERS

Hamm is one of only two women and two Americans named to the FIFA 100—a list of the greatest living soccer players in the world.

Henie was also a movie star. She starred in 10 movies and was one of the highest paid actresses during her career.

SONJA HENIE

FIGURE SKATING

Sonja Henie was born in Oslo, Norway. She got her first pair of ice skates when she was just six. By the time she was 10, she was the best in her country.

In 1924, Henie was in her first Olympics. She was only 11! Competing against older skaters, she finished in last place. She came back four years later and won the gold medal. She added golds in 1932 and 1936—three in a row! Nicknamed the "Ice Queen of Norway," Henie skated like a powerful ballerina. She was one of the first female skaters to do athletic tricks like spins and jumps. Up until then, only men were doing those moves. She made every move seem easy and graceful.

Henie became a pro skater after the 1936 Olympics. She performed in sold-out skating shows all over the United States. She finally retired in 1956.

NUMBERS, NUMBERS

Henie won six European titles (1931-1936) and 10 world titles (1927-1936). Those 10 straight world titles remain a record.

JACKIE JOYNER-KERSEE

TRACK AND FIELD

Many called this track star the world's greatest female athlete. Jackie Joyner-Kersee was fast, strong, agile, and graceful. On the track, she was almost unbeatable.

Joyner-Kersee grew up in St. Louis, Missouri. She went to college at UCLA. There she played basketball and ran track. She was such a great all-around athlete, her track coach found her the perfect sport—the **heptathlon**. That sport includes seven running, jumping, and throwing events! Joyner-Kersee was the first ever to win back-to-back gold medals in the Olympic heptathlon. She won in 1988 and 1992. She also won the 1988 Olympic gold in long jump. And she won a heptathlon silver in 1984, plus two long jump bronze medals.

She still holds the heptathlon world record with 7,291 points. In 2004, she was inducted into the USA Track and Field Hall of Fame.

Sports Illustrated For Women magazine named Joyner-Kersee the greatest female athlete of all time.

NUMBERS, NUMBERS

Only three athletes have ever topped 7,000 points in the heptathlon. Joyner-Kersee did so six times.

KATIE LEDECKY

SWIMMING

Before Katie Ledecky turned 20, she was already a five-time Olympic gold medalist. She also had 14 world championships. That was a world record for female swimmers!

Ledecky grew up in Bethesda, Maryland. She began swimming for a team at six years old. She competed in her first Olympics in 2012, when she was 15. There she won her first gold medal in the 800-meter **freestyle**. Four years later, she won four more golds.

What is the key to her swimming success? First, she never stops practicing. If she isn't in the pool, she feels like a fish out of water. Second, she holds nothing back. As soon as she dives off the block, she goes as hard as she can. "I'm always afraid I'll get to the end and have too much left," she said. Still swimming today, she might still have some gold left in her!

Ledecky won gold medals in three freestyle races at the 2016 Games. She was the first Olympic swimmer to do that since 1968.

NUMBERS, NUMBERS

Ledecky started at Stanford University in 2016. Swimming for the school, she set 12 college records and nine American records.

LISA LESLIE

BASKETBALL

Leslie was elected into the Naismith Memorial Basketball Hall of Fame in 2015.

Lisa Leslie was the first player to dunk in a Women's National Basketball Association (WNBA) game. A 6-5 **center**, she was one of the most dominating basketball players ever.

Early on Leslie was heads above the crowd. In sixth grade, she stood six feet tall and wore size 12 shoes. She was the top high school player in the nation. She later played at the University of Southern California. She was named the top college player in 1994.

Leslie played in four Olympic Games (1996, 2000, 2004, 2008). She won gold medals in all of them. She played for the Los Angeles Sparks and was named WNBA MVP three times. She led thc Sparks to titles in 2001 and 2002.

"It's not our fault that we were born girls," Leslie used to say. "We just want to play, too. Is that too much to ask? I don't think so."

NUMBERS, NUMBERS

As a high school senior in California, Leslie scored 101 points in one half of a basketball game.

ANNIKA SORENSTAM

GOLF

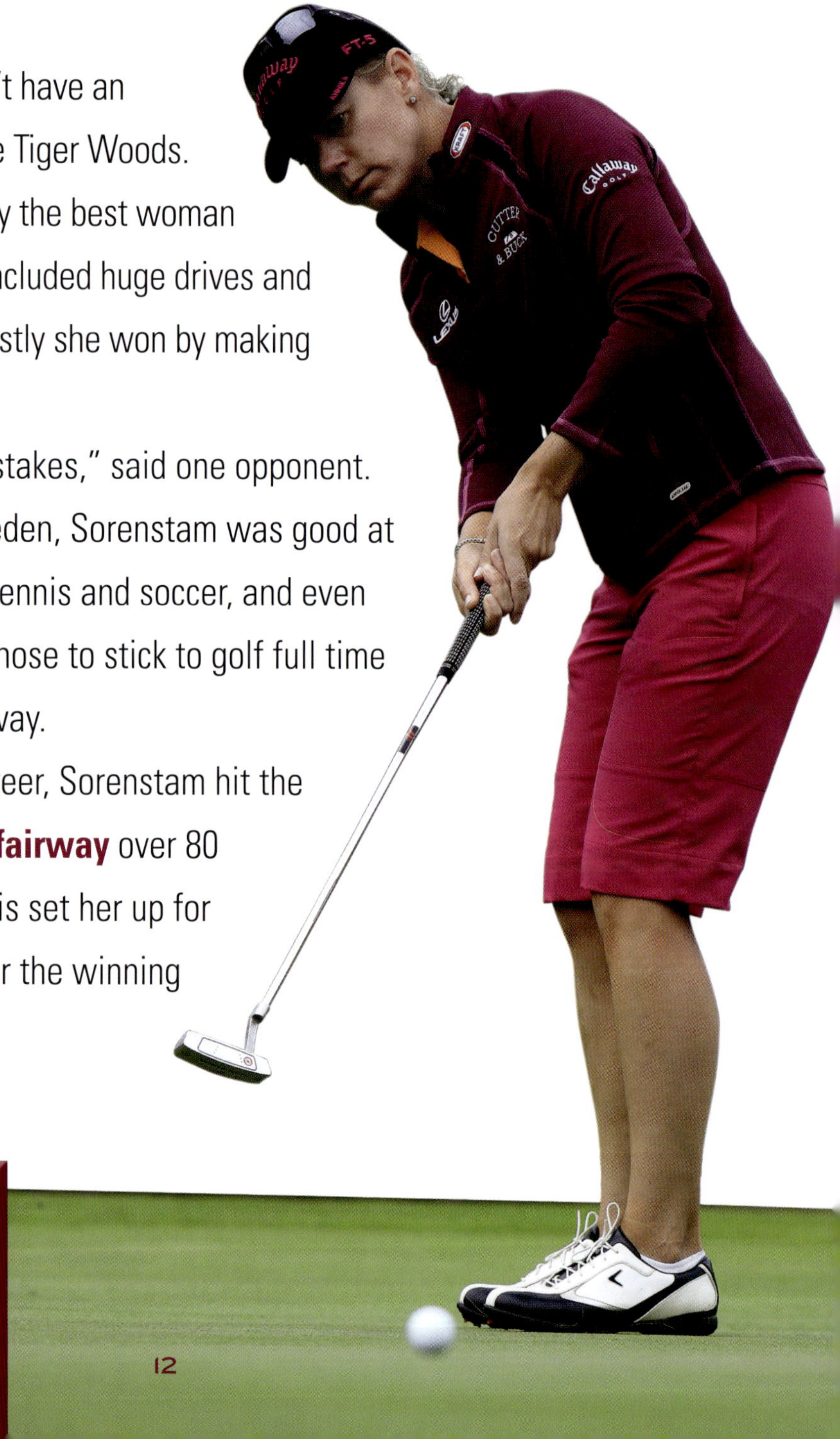

Annika Sorenstam didn't have an awesome nickname like Tiger Woods. Still, she is still probably the best woman golfer ever. Her game included huge drives and unbelievable **putts**. Mostly she won by making smart decisions.

"She makes no mistakes," said one opponent.

Growing up in Sweden, Sorenstam was good at all sports. She played tennis and soccer, and even skied. At age 12, she chose to stick to golf full time and was a star right away.

Throughout her career, Sorenstam hit the ball straight down the **fairway** over 80 percent of the time. This set her up for easy putts and gave her the winning edge. She won—a lot.

NUMBERS, NUMBERS

When Sorenstam retired in 2008, she had earned $22.6 million. That's the most ever by an LPGA player.

When she retired in 2008, she had won 90 tournaments as a pro. That's the most by a female golfer. She also was named the LPGA Player of the Year a record eight times.

In 2003, Sorenstam played against men at a PGA event. She didn't finish among the leaders, but she competed like she belonged.

"Annika can no longer be looked at as a female golfer," one golf writer said after the event. "Now she is simply a golfer."

Sorenstam won 10 of women's golf's major tournaments. She is also the only woman ever to shoot a score of 59 in one pro round.

LINDSEY VONN

SKIING

When most kids were taking their first steps, Lindsey Vonn was skiing. Born in Minnesota in 1984, Vonn hit the slopes at age three. She competed in her first Olympics at 18 in 2002. In her third Olympics in 2010, she won the downhill gold. She was the first U.S. female skier to win that difficult event. Vonn also won a bronze medal in the **supergiant slalom** (Super G) at those Games.

Pro skiers take part in World Cup races. Vonn has won four overall World Cup titles, only one of two women to do so. She also has won a record 20 crystal globes, which are awarded to skiers with season titles on the World Cup circuit.

For winning a race in France, Vonn was awarded a live cow!

Through the 2018 season, Vonn had won 81 World Cup races. That's second all-time among all skiers, male or female.

Vonn reaches speeds of up to 75 miles per hour when she skis. Skiing this fast can be dangerous and Vonn has been injured a lot during her career. She missed the 2014 Olympics because of injury, but returned in time for the 2018 Games, where she won a bronze in the downhill. She has the strength and the desire to fight back time and again. "I'm never tired of winning," Vonn said. "And I'm never tired of skiing."

NUMBERS, NUMBERS

Vonn's World Cup Wins

Event	Wins
Downhill	39
Super G	27
Giant Slalom	4
Super Combined	5
Slalom	2

SERENA WILLIAMS

TENNIS

With her bulging muscles and wicked serve, Serena Williams has dominated women's tennis. No other woman in the history of the sport is more athletic or intense than her.

Growing up in Compton, California, Williams started playing tennis by age three. By age nine, her family moved to Florida. That was so Serena and her older sister Venus could attend a tennis academy. Their father, Richard, always dreamed his girls would be stars.

Williams played her first pro match at age 14. Four years later, in 1999, she won her first U.S. Open title.

Williams has earned more than $84.5 million during her tennis career. That's twice more than any other female player.

Williams has won more Grand Slam titles (39) in singles, doubles, and mixed doubles than any other player. She has also won the second most Grand Slam singles tournaments (23).

Williams was ranked as the No. 1 player in the world for 186 weeks in 2016. That was tied for the longest streak for any woman. Williams has also won four Olympic gold medals in tennis. She earned the 2000 singles gold. Three times, she teamed with sister Venus to win golds in doubles!

Williams earned $29 million in prize money and endorsements in 2016, making her the highest paid female athlete that year. She has become a role model for women everywhere!

NUMBERS, NUMBERS

Williams is the only tennis player to ever win 10 Grand Slam singles titles in two different decades.

BABE DIDRIKSON ZAHARIAS

TRACK AND FIELD • BASKETBALL • GOLF

Babe Didrikson Zaharias did it all . . . and did it all better than most. She was born Mildred Ella Didrikson. Early on, she got the nickname "Babe." She was an amazing athlete before women were encouraged to be athletes at all. She played baseball, volleyball, tennis, and one of her favorites, basketball. She was simply a natural at running fast and jumping high.

Zaharias first made a big mark in track and field. At the 1932 Olympics, she won gold in the javelin throw and the high hurdles. She was second in the high jump. She wasn't done competing though!

After the Games, Zaharias traveled around the country with an all-star basketball team. They beat teams at every level.

In the 1932 Olympics, athletes were only allowed to compete in three track and field events. So it's likely Babe could have won even more medals if given the chance.

When she was off the court, she was even a star at pocket billiards (also called pool) and bowling. What was next for this star? Golf!

Zaharias won three U.S. Women's Open championships. Those were among her 31 LPGA tournament wins.

In 2000, *Sports Illustrated* magazine listed the top 100 athletes of the 20th century. This amazing all-sport superstar was the only woman on the list.

NUMBERS, NUMBERS

In 1999, the *Associated Press* and ESPN named Babe one of the Top 10 Greatest Athletes of the 20th Century.

YOUR TOP TEN!

In this book, we listed our Top 10. We gave you some facts and information about each athlete. Now it's your turn to rank the athletes in order. Find a pen and paper. Make your own list! Who should be named the greatest woman athlete of all time? How about your other nine choices? In your opinion, which athletes are missing from this book? Who would you include? It's your call!

Remember, there are no wrong answers. Every fan might have different choices. Every fan should be able to back up their choices, though. If you need more information, go to the library or online to learn more. Then discuss the choices with your friends!

THINK ABOUT THIS . . .

Here are some things to think about when making your own Top 10 list:

- Did she dominate her sport for an extended period of time?
- Did she break a lot of records? Do the records still stand today?
- Did the athlete have to fight for women to play sports in the first place?
- When did she compete? Has sports for women changed over time?

435

SPORTS GLOSSARY

center (SENN-ter) in basketball, the position that plays closest to the basket

documentary (dok-you-MENN-ter-ee) a true film

fairway (FAIR-wey) the part of the golf course where the grass is cut short between the tee and the putting greens

freestyle (FREE-styl) a swimming stroke in which the arms windmill around and the legs do a flutter kick

Grand Slam (GRAND SLAM) winning all four major tennis tournaments (Australian Open, the French Open, Wimbledon, and the US Open) in one year

heptathlon (hep-TATH-lon) seven different track and field events over two days (100-meter hurdles, high jump, shot put, 200-meters on the first day; long jump, javelin throw, and 800-meters on the second day)

penalty shootout (PENN-ul-tee SHOOT-owt) at the end of some tie soccer games, teams take five shots from 12 yards out; the team that makes the most goals wins

putts (PUTZ) short taps or hits of the golf ball taken on the flat grass area called a green

super-giant slalom (SOO-per JY-unt SLAH-lum) a skiing race when the skier has to go around poles. The course is long and wide.

FIND OUT MORE

IN THE LIBRARY

Buckley, James Jr. *Katie Ledecky: Amazing Americans.* New York, NY: Bearport Publishing, 2017.

Ignotofsky, Rachel. *Women in Sports: 50 Fearless Athletes Who Played to Win.* Berkeley, California: Ten Speed Press, 2017.

Knudson, R.R. *Babe Didrikson: Athlete of the Century.* New York, NY: Puffin Books, 2015.

ON THE WEB

Visit our Web site for links about Top 10 women athletes: **childsworld.com/links**

Note to Parents, Teachers, and Librarians: We routinely verify our Web links to make sure they are safe and active sites. So encourage your readers to check them out!

INDEX

ABOUT THE AUTHOR

Ellen Labrecque was an editor and writer for *Sports Illustrated Kids* magazine. She has written close to 100 books for young readers, many on sports, including some in *The New York Times*-bestselling "Who Was…?" series. She lives in Yardley, Pennsylvania, and loves to run, and play basketball and tennis.